ST. MARY PARISH LIBRARY

3 3446 00278 7121

XF GRA
Gravel, Geary.
Batman and Mr. Freeze /

S0-BIW-408

BATMAN®

and

MR. FREEZE™

Written by Geary Gravel
Based on the script, *Deep Freeze*, by Paul Dini
Illustrated by Brandon Kruse, Aluir Amâncio, and Glen Murakami
Batman created by Bob Kane

ST. MARY PARISH LIBRARY
FRANKLIN, LOUISIANA
70538

A GOLDEN BOOK • NEW YORK
Golden Books Publishing Company, Inc., Racine, Wisconsin 53404

Batman and all related characters and indicia are the property of DC Comics. © 1997. All rights reserved. Printed in the U.S.A. No part of this book may be reproduced or copied in any form without written permission from the copyright owner. All other trademarks are the property of Golden Books Publishing Company, Inc. Library of Congress Catalog Card Number: 95-81520 ISBN: 0-307-12938-1   A MCMXCVII

Mr. Freeze was a brilliant scientist and inventor. One day he and his wife, Nora, were caught in a laboratory explosion. Mr. Freeze's body chemistry was so changed by the explosion that he could survive only by wearing a special cold suit that controlled his temperature. Nora was never found.

Mr. Freeze mourned the loss of his beloved wife—but soon his grief turned to anger. Using an ice gun he'd invented, he went on a crime spree.

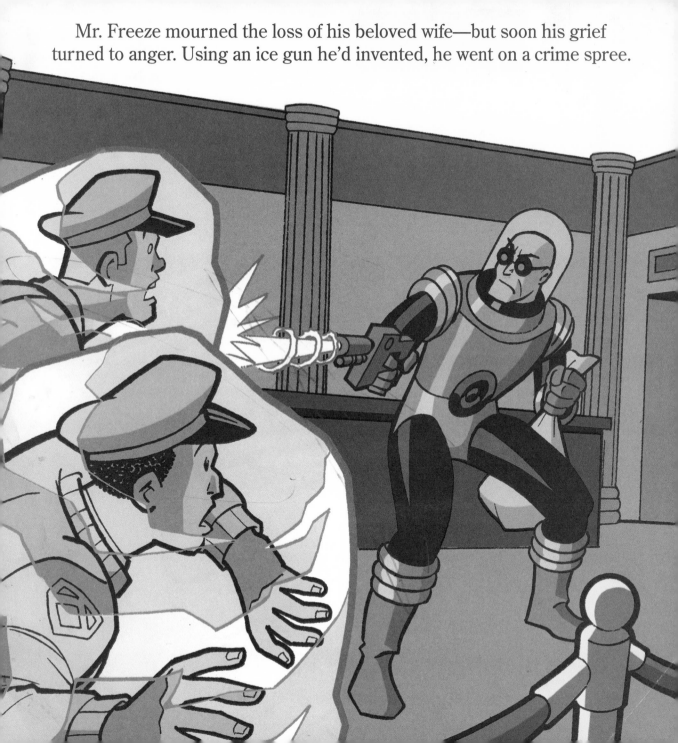

But Batman and Robin soon stopped Mr. Freeze, and he was sent to Arkham Asylum. There he remained until he was kidnapped by a robot!

Later in the Batcave, Batman and Robin watched the kidnapping on a video that the police had supplied. "That looks like a robot from Oceana, the floating city that Grant Walker built," Robin said.

"Get the Batboat," said Batman. "We're going to Oceana."

Meanwhile, the robot delivered Mr. Freeze to Walker. "I've brought you here to complete my giant ice cannon," said Walker.

"I'm not interested in your inventions," said Mr. Freeze.

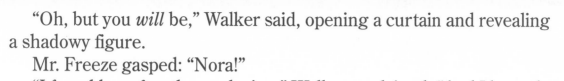

"Oh, but you *will* be," Walker said, opening a curtain and revealing a shadowy figure.

Mr. Freeze gasped: "Nora!"

"I found her after the explosion," Walker explained. "And I have the technology to revive her—but only if you help me with the cannon!"

"Nora," Mr. Freeze whispered. "I'd do *anything* for her."

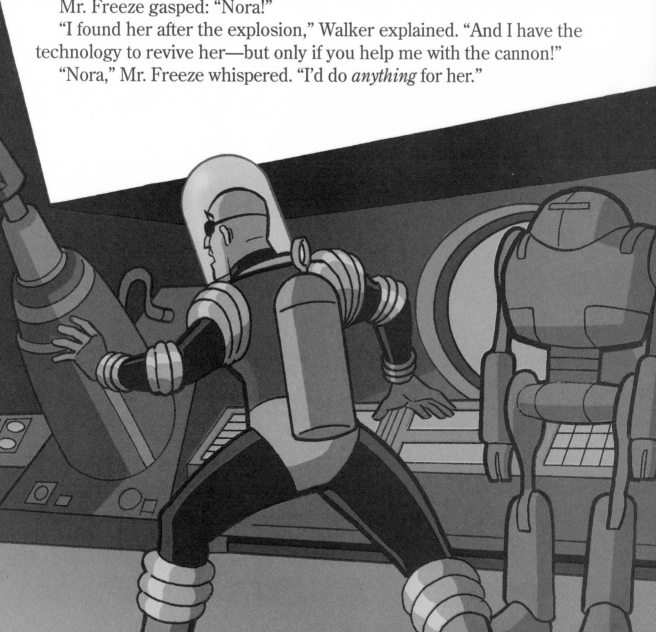

Just then, an alarm sounded.

"Your old enemies, Batman and Robin, have arrived," Walker told Mr. Freeze. "My sharkbots will take care of them while you work on the ice cannon."

"Look out!" Robin yelled as the sharkbots approached.

"Jump, Robin!" Batman cried. Using Batarangs, the duo swung to safety. As the sharkbots destroyed the Batboat, Batman and Robin located a secret entrance to Oceana.

Once inside Oceana, Batman and Robin found their way to the main office.

"What's this?" Robin wondered, looking at a model of Oceana surrounded by ice. "Is Walker building a city at the North Pole?"

"Not quite," answered Walker, surprising them. "It's a model of my new world. Thanks to Mr. Freeze's genius, my ice cannon is complete. Now I can freeze everything outside Oceana and live here with my robots and friends."

Walker signaled Mr. Freeze to fire his ice gun. Batman and Robin were instantly trapped!

"I've done all you've asked," Mr. Freeze said to Walker. "The cannon is ready. Now revive Nora."

"*After* I use the ice cannon!" shouted Walker, running from the room.

"You must free us," Batman urged Mr. Freeze. "Think! Would Nora want to live in a frozen world you helped create?"

Realizing Batman was right, Mr. Freeze summoned his amazing strength and smashed the ice.

Batman and Robin raced to the control room to stop Walker. Seconds later, Mr. Freeze rushed in and changed the setting on the ice cannon. An alarm sounded!

"You fool!" Walker screamed. "You've activated the self-destruct. We'll be blown out of the water!"

Sparks flew from the cannon. The floor buckled.
Walker screamed as he and the cannon crashed
through the opening in the floor.

"We have to get out of here!" yelled Batman.

"No," shouted Mr. Freeze. "I won't leave without Nora."

Robin tried to grab Mr. Freeze, but the villain froze him with the ice gun. Then the entire floor collapsed, and Mr. Freeze disappeared.

Batman carried his frozen partner onto a boat at the docks. As they sped to safety, Oceana crumbled behind them.

Back in the Batcave, Robin thawed out slowly. "We stopped Walker's plan to freeze the world," he said.

"But what about Mr. Freeze?" asked Alfred the butler.

"Mr. Freeze won't stop until he and his wife are together again," said Batman. "I'm sure we haven't seen the last of him."

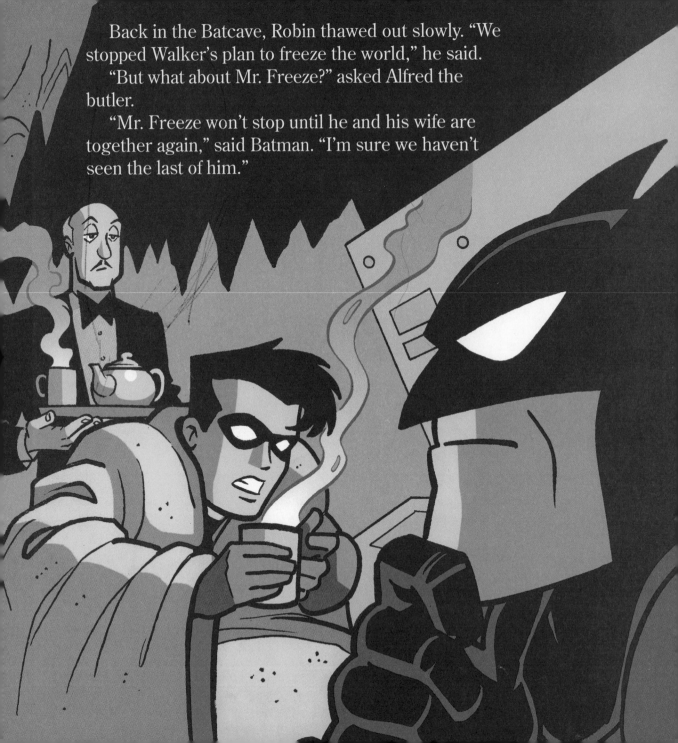